TERRIFYING TALES

NINE STORIES OF SPINE-TINGLING SUSPENSE

RETOLD BY NICOLA BAXTER
ILLUSTRATED BY GRAHAM HOWELLS
AND DAVID LEITH

ARMADILLO

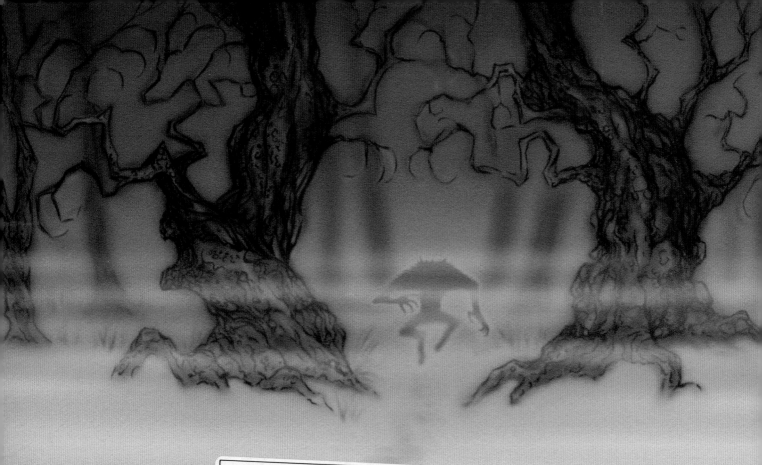

Contents

Dracula

It is the eve of St George's Day. Do you not know that tonight, when the clock strikes midnight, all the evil things in the world will have full sway? Do you know where you are going, and what you are going to?" an old woman asked Jonathan Harker. He was staying the night at an inn in remote Transylvania, on his way to meet the Count at Dracula Castle.

The next day, the he set off on the last part of his journey. Carried by coach through wild, mountainous countryside, as night fell, he was still not prepared for his first sight of the feared castle.

For the first part of the journey, Harker had company. Local peasants, brightly dressed, were also taking the coach. They were friendly enough, although he did not speak their language, but they seemed to be in fear of his destination and what might befall him.

As arranged, Harker alighted at the end of a rocky mountain pass to await a coach sent from his host to take him the rest of the way. There were dark, rolling clouds overhead, and the air was heavy with an oppressive sense of thunder. From out of the blackness, a caleche drawn by four coal-black horses arrived, driven by a tall, bearded man, his face shadowed by a great black hat. Only his eyes were visible, and they seemed to gleam red in the lamplight.

With some misgivings, Harker climbed into the caleche, which hurtled away into the darkness. It was close to midnight. Suddenly, from somewhere close to the lonely road, a dog began to howl, followed by another and then another, until the caleche appeared to be surrounded by the mournful, fearsome sound. Then, far off in the distance, a sharper howling began in answer. Wolves!

Harker became increasingly unnerved, especially as the driver stopped from time to time and disappeared into the forest and the darkness. On one such occasion, the horses began to tremble and scream with fright. To his horror, Harker saw that the caleche was surrounded by a ring of wolves, howling in the moonlight. In his terror, Harker believed himself doomed, but the coachman returned and seemed to banish the wolves by some mysterious power.

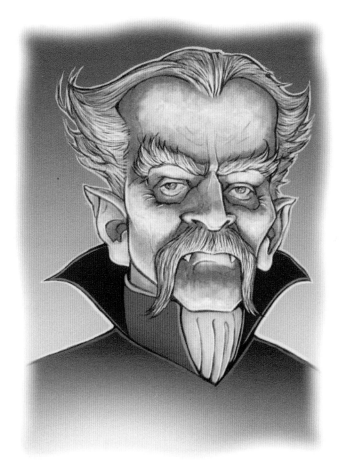

The road wound upward. At last, the caleche came to a stop in the courtyard of a vast, ruined castle. There was no light from its tall windows, and the broken battlements were silhouetted menacingly against the brooding sky.

The nervous passenger stood before the great wooden door of the castle. From within came the sound of chains being unfastened and bolts drawn back. Slowly, the door creaked open, revealing a tall old man with a long white moustache, dressed from head to foot in black. He held a lamp in his hand, and strange shadows flickered around him as he welcomed Harker into the castle. It was the Count himself.

Inside, Harker felt his spirits lifting. Newly qualified as a solicitor, he had come from Exeter, England, to advise the Count on the purchase of some property in London. This was his first time in so wild a part of the world, for the Carpathian Mountains in those days were known to shelter an almost medieval way of life. But the young man found himself shown to a comfortable, warm and well-lit suite of rooms, where good food and wine were laid out. The Count himself waited on his guest. Although much cheered, Harker could not help but notice the cruel cast of the Count's face, his peculiarly sharp teeth and his pointed finger nails.

Suddenly, the sound of howling wolves again filled the air, although from far away. The Count's eyes gleamed, "Listen to them, the children of the night. What music they make!" he said.

Telling his visitor that he would be away until the afternoon of the following day, the Count left Harker to rest, bidding him sleep as late as he wished. The young man slept well and was delighted to find a breakfast laid out ready for him when he rose late on the following day. He noticed that the rooms were richly furnished in an old-fashioned style and that, curiously, there were no mirrors anywhere.

As dusk fell, Harker was once again joined by the Count, who, although he did not join his guest in his meals, was happy to talk, telling of the proud and bloody history of his family. He wished, too, to speak of the property that Harker's firm had found for him. The young man described it, and the Count seemed well pleased by its isolation and the fact that it was old and large. "I love the shade and the shadow," said the old man, "and would be alone with my thoughts when I may." Something about his words seemed distinctly sinister.

Days passed, each recorded in Harker's secret journal. On the second day, using his pocket shaving mirror, the solicitor was shocked when the Count came up behind him and surprised him. There had been no image of the Count in the mirror! The jolt caused Harker to cut himself. Seeing the blood, the Count's eyes gleamed demonically, and his hands reached involuntarily for the young man's throat. At the touch of the crucifix given to Harker by the old woman at the inn, the Count withdrew with a shudder, however.

It soon began to dawn on the young man that he never saw another living soul in the castle. He became convinced that there were no servants. The Count was tending to his needs himself. And yet he never saw his host by the light of day. Somehow, both Harker and the Count were leading a nocturnal existence, talking far into the night but never meeting by day. The strain of it began to tell on the young man. He longed for home and the company of his fiancée Mina. His discomfort increased when he found that he was locked into the castle, with no means of escape. Suspecting, perhaps, that his visitor had been attempting to wander, the Count warned him never to sleep anywhere but in his own rooms and hinted at dark consequences should he disobey.

One night, after the Count had left him, Harker went up a small stone stair that led to a chamber with a mullioned window opening to the south. The moon was so bright that he could see clearly the stonework of the castle. A slight movement made Harker look out farther. The Count's own rooms, he calculated, were below and to the left. To the young man's horror, he saw the Count himself emerging from his window, wrapped in a great, black cape. He seemed to creep like some kind of animal down the sheer wall, disappearing into the darkness below.

Shortly after this, a further horror awaited the young man, who once more ventured out of his rooms and found an ancient chamber, decorated beautifully in the style of several centuries before. As he lay there on a couch, three beautiful women appeared in the moonlight, their skins pale and their eyes glowing almost red in the gloom. Two were dark and one was fair, and the young man was strongly attracted to them, although a sense of terror grew in him as the fair one neared him. He saw her licking her red lips, which opened over white, pointed teeth, as she bent over him to kiss his naked throat.

The moment was shattered by the arrival of the Count, his eyes burning with fury. He pushed the women back and told them that Harker was his own until he had finished with him. "Are we to have nothing tonight?" asked one of the women. In answer, the Count threw down a bag on to the floor. Something living squirmed within it and, as the women fell upon it, Harker almost thought he heard the terrified cry of a child.

By now, Harker believed himself to be doomed. When the Count asked him to write postdated letters, telling of his journey home, he was convinced that his last days had come. Still, at night, he watched from the window and saw the Count leaving his room in that ghastly manner. One night, there were worse horrors. A woman came into the courtyard and screamed up at the windows for the return of her child. Her cries were heart-rending, but the Count merely looked from his window and whispered into the night air. As if in answer, a massive pack of wolves streamed into the courtyard. When they left, their fangs dripping, there was no sign of the desperate woman.

Feeling that he had nothing to lose, Harker decided on a desperate course of action. Realizing that he never saw the Count in daylight, he decided to climb down the castle walls as he saw his host do. The descent was perilous but successful. Harker climbed into the Count's room and found it deserted, furnished in the style of three hundred years before. Following a narrow passage, he stumbled across the vaults of a ruined chapel, surrounded by the graves of the Count's ancestors. Several huge wooden boxes, filled with earth, stood open on the floor. In one of them, the Count himself lay as if dead. Harker knew for sure now that the Count was no ordinary mortal.

When the Count finally told Harker that he would shortly be able to leave, the young man was deeply suspicious. He determined to find his host by daylight once more and to search his body for the key to the outer door. Perhaps there was one last chance of escape.

The following day, Harker once more descended to the vaults. This time, the lid of the box was in position, but the young man wrenched it off. A horrifying sight met his eyes. There lay the Count as before, but this time he looked as if he had dined well. Blood dripped from his red lips and the corners of his mouth. He looked younger. His white hair was now darker and his skin was smooth and gorged with blood.

With a feeling of sick horror, Harker's first instinct was to attempt to rid the world of such a monster. He grasped the nearest thing to hand – a shovel left from the filling of the boxes – and brought it down upon the vile face of the Count. As he did so, the head turned, and the eyes of the vampire fixed themselves on his terrified assailant. Although the blow caused a gash that would have killed a mortal man, the last thing that Harker saw as the lid of the box fell shut was the lips of Dracula drawn back in a hellish, never-to-be-forgotten grin of sheer evil.

The story of Dracula is told in a novel of the same name, written by Bram Stoker, an Irish author who lived between 1847 and 1912. Some say that he based his "hero" on a fifteenth-century Romanian prince. The historical Dracula certainly had a reputation for appalling cruelty (he was also known as Vlad the Impaler), but there is no record linking him with vampirism.

The idea of the "undead", who drink the blood of the living, has, however, been around for centuries. One gruesome explanation is that in the days before brain scans and heart monitors, some unfortunate people in comas were thought to be dead and were buried alive. Occasionally these coffins would later be reopened, revealing the horror of a corpse with a bloody face and hands where it had clawed and bitten at the coffin lid in an attempt to escape.

The Curse of the Mummy

Can it ever be right to rob the grave of another human being, taking everything – even his body – from its final resting place? Even the least superstitious grave-robber must sometimes feel uneasy. Yet tombs are violated every day in the name of science.

In the nineteenth century, archaeologists became fascinated by ancient Egypt. It was tantalizing to know that in the Valley of the Kings, across the Nile from the city once known as Thebes, the tombs of the greatest Pharaohs lay hidden, waiting to be discovered.

It was known that these mighty rulers had been entombed surrounded by untold treasures, taking with them into the afterlife the luxury and beauty they had known in life on earth.

A young Englishman named Howard Carter arrived in Egypt in 1891. For years he worked, becoming ever more convinced that the tomb of the boy king, Tutankhamun, was waiting to be found. Although local workers were fairly cheap, such expeditions were costly and time-consuming. Carter was lucky to have the backing of wealthy Lord Carnarvon, but after years of fruitless effort, Carnarvon called his protégé home, unwilling to throw more money into a hopeless quest.

Carter, however, had lost none of his passion. He was able to convince his patron to fund one more season's digging.

When cultures meet, there is often confusion and misunderstanding. Carter took with him on his return to Egypt a yellow canary. To Reis Ahmed, Carter's Egyptian foreman, it had great significance. "A golden bird!" he cried. "It will lead us to the tomb!"

Sure enough, on 4 November 1922, the first of fifteen steps, leading to a sealed doorway, was found. The name inscribed on the door made Carter's heart leap. It was Tutankhamun. Some say that there was also something else written outside the tomb: Death shall come on swift wings to him who disturbs the peace of the King. In fact, no evidence for this has been found, but something else happened that Carter's workmen thought was equally ominous. That night, Carter's servant told him that the golden bird (the canary) had been killed by a cobra. "The serpent of the Pharaoh killed the bird because it led us to his tomb!" the terrified man cried. "Do not enter the tomb!"

Carter was not a superstitious man. He telegraphed his patron and tried to stifle his impatience as he waited for him to arrive. On 26 November, with Lord Carnarvon just behind him, Carter made a small hole in the ancient, sealed door. By the flickering light of a candle, he peered into a room that had not been opened for thousands of years.

"Can you see anything?" asked the nobleman.

"Yes, wonderful things!" the awe-struck archaeologist replied.

The whole world has now seen those wonderful things. Three gold coffins, one inside the other, contained the mummy of the boy king. His golden mask has become famous the world over.

More recently still, examination of the body of Tutankhamun has revealed a more sinister secret. It seems that the boy king suffered from spinal problems all his short life, and it is more than likely that he met his death by murder.

Back in the 1920s, a sinister atmosphere surrounded the tomb's discovery, too...

Not long after the tomb was opened, Lord Carnarvon was taken seriously ill. An insect bite on his cheek became infected. Rushed back to Cairo, the nobleman received every attention, to no avail. A few days later, at the age of 57, he died. It is said that at the same moment, the lights of Cairo also flickered and died, as a power cut engulfed the city.

Back in England, that very evening, Lord Carnarvon's best-loved dog howled once and dropped, lifeless, to the ground.

News of the mummy's curse was soon whispered everywhere. More and more strange happenings added to the sense of doom. When Tutankhamun's mummy was finally unwrapped in 1925, it was found to have a wound upon the face exactly where Lord Carnarvon had been bitten.

The man who actually opened Tutankhamun's tomb, and should have had more reason to fear the curse than anyone, never believed in it. He died of natural causes at the age of 66.

However, in 1999, Gotthard Kramer, a German microbiologist, identified several dangerous would spores in the wrappings of Egyptian mummies, for this reason, archaeologists today wear masks and protective clothing when examining the contents of ancient tombs.

As usual, it is ignorance of the legacies of the past, not the past itself, that can endanger future generations. The curse of the boy king was perhaps more natural than supernatural after all.

The Body Snatchers

As the condemned man stood upon the scaffold, the nightmare sight that met his eyes was of hundreds of jeering onlookers, people for whom his death would be mere entertainment. Nearer to the platform stood two men whose expressions were no less eager. They horrified the convicted felon even more. They would be taking his body away, not for burial, but to be cut and dismembered by students at a local medical school. It was a fate to be feared, for, at the Day of Judgement, how could a body rise to meet its maker severed limb from limb?

In nineteenth century Britain, the number of medical students was rising faster than the number of executed criminals. No decent person would permit his or her body to be dissected after death. There was a distinct shortage of available corpses.

Where there is a shortage, it is never long before someone with an eye for business thinks of a way to supply the market. It occurred to more than one ne'er-do-well that the place to find a body was … a graveyard.

At dead of night, towns and cities in those days were dark indeed. Only a few flickering lamps gave an eerie glow to street corners or outside important homes. In the back streets, the shadows that slipped through the narrow alleys and stinking yards had no honest business to transact. Those same shadows slid over the walls and railings of the graveyards, carrying picks and shovels wrapped in rags. Posting lookouts to warn of the approach of the night-watchman, they set about their gruesome task.

Long before dawn turned the darkness to a sickly grey, newly dug graves had been refilled. No sorrowing mourner, standing by the graveside, would guess that the coffin far below was empty, and his dearly loved wife, mother or child under a student's knife on the other side of the city.

If medical professors and their students were sometimes suspicious about the condition of the corpses they received, they said nothing. After all, in a very short time, the bodies became horrifically unrecognizable. For the grave-robbers, it was a very lucrative trade.

Perhaps it was inevitable that sooner or later someone would think of an even more cost-effective way to satisfy the medical schools' needs.

William Burke and William Hare both came from Ireland, although they did not know each other there. Both worked at various manual jobs before meeting by chance in Edinburgh. Burke ran a boarding house with his common-law wife Margaret Logue. Hare had taken up with a woman called Helen McDougal. The pair soon moved into the boarding house themselves.

One of Hare's lodgers was an army veteran called Donald. In November 1827, Donald died at the boarding house. Hare was distraught, but not because he was grieving for the old man. The fact was that Donald owed £4 in rent and there was now no chance for Hare to retrieve it. Or was there?

As Donald lay in his coffin, Hare came up with a plan. Helped by Burke, he removed the corpse and filled the box with a sack of bark before sealing it. When the authorities came to take the coffin away, the body of Donald remained in the house.

Now Burke and Hare had a very saleable item. They made their way to the lecture rooms of Professor Robert Knox, whose staff suggested they bring the body after dark. Later that night, Burke and Hare hurried through the streets, carrying a heavy sack. At Knox's premises, the body was removed. Donald's fixed, pale features were once again revealed in the lamplight. To their delight, Burke and Hare received £7 for the former lodger.

It must have been on the journey
back to the boarding house that the
unscrupulous pair realized that
there was an even easier way
to make money.

A few days later, Joseph, who also had the misfortune to live in
Hare's boarding house, fell ill. Although his illness was fairly minor, Burke
and Hare decided that he had suffered enough. They kindly offered him
glass after glass of whisky, until Joseph was more or less unconscious.
Then, while one man held Joseph down, the other suffocated him. Once
again, Professor Knox received a visit. With no incriminating marks on
the body, and clear evidence of drunkenness in the deceased, no one was
suspicious about the death. Burke and Hare received their payment.
It was a long, cold winter, but the other residents of the
boarding house proved to be annoyingly healthy. Burke
and Hare were obliged to go further afield. In
February, William Hare came across an elderly lady
on her way home with her pension money. She
accepted Hare's invitation to rest and
enjoy a drink at his boarding house
before she set out for home. Burke
and Helen McDougal plied the old
woman, called Abigail Simpson,
with whisky and persuaded her to
stay the night. In the morning,
after a little more whisky, they
sent her on a far longer
journey than she had planned.

That evening, Burke and Hare manhandled a tea chest through the Edinburgh streets. Professor Knox himself met them and inspected its contents. He noticed that the corpse was extraordinarily "fresh", and paid £10 for it.

Many, many times over the next few months, Burke and Hare made deliveries to Professor Knox. They drank away most of the money they received, so they were always looking for new victims. It seems very likely that their womenfolk helped to keep them in the style to which they had become accustomed.

Burke and Helen McDougal now had their own rooms nearby. On the night of Halloween, when the dead are said to revisit the living, Burke's last murder did indeed come back to haunt him. That morning, he had met an old Irish woman in an inn. She was Mary Docherty, and she was only too happy to come back to Burke's lodgings to carry on drinking. A couple called James and Ann Gray were staying there at the time, but they agreed to go and stay at Hare's boarding house that night instead. From the moment they left, Mary Docherty's fate was sealed.

The next morning, the Grays returned to be told that the visitor had already left. But when Ann Gray happened to go near the spare bed, Burke yelled at her to stay away. Later that day, finding themselves alone for a moment, the Grays looked under the bed. They found that Mary Docherty was still in residence.

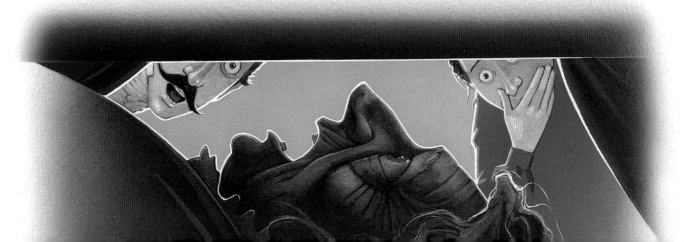

The Grays rushed off to find a policeman, but Burke had time to cover his tracks. When the constabulary arrived, there was no body, just an innocent-looking couple. Helen and William were parted and individually questioned. It was here that they made their big mistake. Helen claimed that Mary Docherty had left at seven the previous evening. Burke said it was seven that morning. When the police, working on a mysterious tip, visited Professor Knox's establishment, they found Mary Docherty, pale and still.

Now the work began of unravelling eleven months of cold, calculated crime. It wasn't easy. Although there was lots of circumstantial evidence about Burke or Hare being seen with various people shortly before they disappeared, there was little actual proof. In the end, Hare was promised immunity from prosecution if he would testify against Burke, which he gladly did.

Burke was executed on 28 January 1829. The scaffold was surrounded by the largest crowd that had ever been seen at an Edinburgh hanging, with wealthy folk as well as paupers crowding to see. There was no feeling of sympathy for the offender, but a joyful mood amongst the crowd. And the fate of Burke's body? He knew it only too well. The next day, a packed audience of medical students watched as Burke's skull was sawn off and his brain dissected. It seemed a fitting end.

William Hare, Helen McDougal and Margaret Logue were all forced to leave Edinburgh to escape from the angry mob. There are stories about their eventual fates, but no real facts. What happened to Professor Knox, however, is known. After his association with Burke and Hare was discovered, his reputation suffered, and medical students dwindled. He failed to find a new post in Edinburgh and moved to London, where he worked in a cancer hospital. He died in 1862.

Monstrous Creation

M aybe human beings differ most greatly from other creatures in their huge desire to push back the barriers to knowledge and discover more about our world and our own human nature. It is an insatiable desire, but it is one that brings fear, too. We both long for knowledge and the power that it brings and shrink from the unknown, which may be more terrifying than anything that is familiar to us now.

The story of Frankenstein opens with the letters of an English explorer on a voyage to the North Pole.

The date is sometime during the eighteenth century, when those icy realms had not yet been explored, but a spirit of exploration filled many hearts in those days, particularly in scientific matters. Robert Walton, the leader of this expedition, wished not only to visit places that had never before been seen by human eyes, but also to investigate the source of the magnetism that caused his compass to point ever northwards.

It was while his ship, heading towards the Pole, was caught fast in pack ice that Walton first sighted, far off, an awesome figure. It was riding on a sledge pulled by dogs, but what struck the Englishman most forcibly was the size of the driver. He seemed almost a giant.

The next morning, there was another surprise. Floating ice brought to the side of the ship another figure, lying close to death in his own snowbound sledge. Just one of his dogs remained alive, and it was only after considerable care and attention on board ship that the emaciated man became strong enough to speak.

When asked why he was journeying in so desolate a spot, the weak and half-crazed man replied, "To seek one who fled from me." Walton rightly guessed that this was the huge figure he had seen the day before. It soon became clear that the stranger was suffering in spirit as well as in body. His despair was all too clear. In the days that followed, he came to trust the Englishman and agreed to tell him his disturbing story.

The stranger's name, it seemed, was Victor Frankenstein, born in Geneva to a prosperous and loving father and his much younger wife. Frankenstein's early life was filled with love and happiness. His two brothers were several years younger than Victor, but before their birth his parents had adopted the orphaned child of a nobleman, Elizabeth Lavenza. Young Frankenstein adored this delightful girl and, in her company and that of his close friend Henry Clerval, passed an idyllic childhood.

Victor was clearly an intelligent boy and enjoyed his studies, which soon led him to consider the deepest mysteries of life itself. At seventeen, he was eager to travel to the University of Ingolstadt to begin his studies of natural philosophy and chemistry in earnest. He was devastated when, on the eve of his departure, his beloved mother became ill and died. His misery at her loss tainted his first months in Ingolstadt, but Victor soon found deep fascination in his studies. After so close an experience of death, it was not perhaps surprising that he began to investigate the secrets of life.

Another man might have shuddered at Victor's obsession. To study the spark of life and what happens when it is extinguished, he observed in the greatest detail the decay of human corpses. After many years of research, he felt that he had found the secret he had been seeking.

So feverish was the young man's search that he barely made contact with his family and friends. He could think only of one thing, and without pausing to consider the consequences, he worked for months to construct a human being from body parts obtained from corpses.

On a rain-lashed night in November, well after midnight, Victor Frankenstein finally succeeded in his mission. Under his fascinated gaze, the eyes of the creature he had made flickered open, and his great limbs began to move.

Frankenstein had taken infinite care to choose for his creation the mightiest features, the blackest hair, the whitest teeth and the brightest eyes, but he was not prepared for the horror of their appearance when combined and triggered into life. Disgusted, disappointed and disturbed, the young scientist fled from the room and spent the rest of the night pacing desperately in the alleys and courtyards of the town.

Early the next morning, Frankenstein was delighted to meet up with his old friend Henry Clerval, who had arrived to study at the university, but Clerval was shocked by the change in his friend. Summoning up the courage to return to his apartment, Frankenstein found that the monster had gone, but he dared not confide in his friend. Run down by months of unceasing work, the scientist fell ill. For weeks, Clerval nursed him, until he was well enough to return home to Geneva.

But Frankenstein's horror was far from over. Just before leaving, he heard that his beloved younger brother, William, had been found strangled in woods near his home. Frankenstein hurried to his family, but on the way could not resist visiting the scene of his brother's murder. Night fell. As the young man walked through the woods, the surrounding mountains were suddenly lit by great flashes of lightning,

and heavy rain began to lash the countryside. In the midst of the tremendous storm, Frankenstein suddenly saw the hideous figure of his creation ahead of him. At once he became convinced that the creature itself was William's killer.

The monster disappeared on the mountain slopes, and Frankenstein headed for home. Here there was misery and despair at the death of a young and beautiful boy, but for Frankenstein there was another horror. Justine Moritz, a good-hearted serving girl who had become part of the household, had been accused of William's murder, The evidence was slight, but in a city eager for vengeance for so foul a deed, it was enough to hang her. For Frankenstein, convinced of the girl's innocence, the trial and execution were torture.

Unable to cope with his guilt and sorrow, Frankenstein fled to the mountains, hoping in solitude and quiet to regain something of his peace of mind. Out walking one day on a massive glacier, he was approached by the one being he most dreaded meeting. Frankenstein's feelings overcame him. "Devil!" cried the young man. "Begone, vile insect! Or rather, stay, that I may trample you to dust! And, oh! That I could, with the extinction of your miserable existence, restore those victims whom you have so diabolically murdered!"

To Frankenstein's astonishment, the monster not only replied, but spoke piteously and powerfully about his condition.

"All men hate the wretched; how, then, must I be hated, who am miserable beyond all living things! ... You purpose to kill me. How dare you sport thus with life? Do your duty towards me, and I will do mine towards you and the rest of mankind. If you will comply with my conditions, I will leave them and you at peace; but if you refuse, I will glut the maw of death, until it be satiated with the blood of your remaining friends. Everywhere I see bliss, from which I alone am irrevocably excluded. I was benevolent and good; misery made me a fiend. Make me happy, and I shall again be virtuous."

A dreary rain began to fall upon the glacier, but the monster's words had touched Frankenstein. He felt his responsibility towards the creature he had made, and followed him to a nearby alpine hut to hear his story.

By the light of a basic fire, the monster told how he became more fully human, learning speech and the meanings of emotions, although deprived of normal human comfort and care. Watching the love between men and women, adults and children, he felt ever more keenly his own isolation. At one point, the unhappy being saved a young girl from drowning in a stream, but a man with a gun, thinking he meant to harm her, fired at the gruesome creature. Alone in the cold forest, the monster had to care for his wound himself, although the pain almost drove him mad. Every event seemed to make his life more intolerable. His hatred of the man who had given him such a life grew and grew.

Eventually, the miserable creature told how he came across William in the woods. The child screamed at the sight of him, although the monster tried to explain that he meant him no harm. Then, fatally, William told his name, meaning to impress his attacker, as he saw it, with the name of his powerful father. At the sound of the name Frankenstein, however, the creature's feelings overcame him. His murder of the innocent boy was an attempt to injure Victor himself, the creator both of the horrifying being and all his miseries.

Finally, the creature told Frankenstein of his demands. In a sense, they were simple and understandable:

"You must create a female for me with whom I can live in the interchange of those sympathies necessary for my being. This you alone can do, and I demand it of you as a right which you must not refuse to concede."

At first, Frankenstein certainly did refuse. But the monster's words had touched him, and he felt a strange compassion for the creature he had created. Finally, he agreed that if the monster would promise to go far away, where no one would ever see him, he would do as he asked.

"I swear," the monster replied, "by the sun, and by the blue sky of heaven, and by the fire of love that burns my heart, that if you grant my prayer, while they exist you shall never behold me again. Fear not that when you are ready I shall appear."

Accompanied by his good friend Henry Clerval, Frankenstein headed for a remote island in the Orkneys to work on his second creation, but doubts about his actions continued to haunt him. What if the female creature hated her mate and he her? Might they not wreak an even greater vengeance on the world in their disappointment? Worse, what if they found in each other all they wished and had children as fearful as themselves? Glancing up, Frankenstein saw his creature through the window, a look of greed and anticipation on his face. In fear and loathing of what he had done, Frankenstein destroyed his work.

Seeing that the scientist was resolute about his decision, the monster delivered a horrifying curse.

"Man! You may hate, but beware! Your hours will pass in dread and misery, and soon the bolt will fall which must ravish from you your happiness forever. I may die, but first you, my tyrant and tormentor, shall curse the sun that gazes on your misery. Beware, for I am fearless and therefore powerful. I will watch with the wiliness of a snake, that I may sting with its venom. I shall be with you on your wedding night."

The very next day, Frankenstein's horrors began anew, when the body of Henry Clerval was discovered with huge finger-marks around his neck. Although at first accused of the crime himself and imprisoned, Frankenstein was at last acquitted. He returned to Geneva, where his marriage to his beloved Elizabeth had long been anticipated.

The marriage took place on a hot, sunny day with great rejoicing, but in Frankenstein's mind one great fear remained. He remembered the monster's curse and felt sure that on his wedding night the creature meant to kill him. As evening drew on, Frankenstein and his bride arrived at Evian, where they were to spend the night. Sending Elizabeth to their room, Frankenstein was determined not to join her until he had some clue as to the intentions of his enemy. In the flickering lamplight, he searched the rooms and corridors of the house, gradually gaining confidence as no sign of the creature was found.

Suddenly, a scream ripped through the air. In an instant, Frankenstein knew his fate. It was Elizabeth, not himself, that the creature intended to harm. He rushed into her room, but it was too late. The beautiful girl lay dead, the marks of the creature's great hands around her neck. Soon afterwards, Frankenstein's father, too, died, broken-hearted.

From that moment, Frankenstein had only one thought: to track the monster down and destroy him. He followed him ever northward, finally chasing him over the Arctic ice by sledge. It was when the ice broke up in a storm, almost killing them both, that Victor Frankenstein met the ship under the command of Robert Walton. Frankenstein's misery was not to continue for long. Weak and despairing, he died soon after.

Later Walton was surprised to hear sounds in the cabin where his body lay. Opening the door he was shocked to see the figure of the monster weeping over his creator.

The creature's last words were to Walton. "Soon I shall die. My spirit will sleep in peace, or if it thinks, it will not surely think thus. Farewell."

So saying, the monster leapt from the window on to an ice raft floating below. The waves carried him away into darkness and distance.

The story of frankenstein was written by Mary Shelley, wife of the poet Percy Bysshe Shelley, and published in 1818. She and her husband were staying with Lord Byron in Switzerland at the time and amused themselves in the evenings by telling frightening stories by the fire. This tale has been popular ever since. In the misery of frankenstein's creation, we can see something of the fears of any human life, and it has sometimes been said that of all the characters in the book, it is the monster who is most truly human.

Sentence of Death

I s it possible to kill a man by turning the power of his own fear against him? Strange tales have been told.

In Darwin, Australia, in the early 1950s, doctors stood over the bed of an Aboriginal Australian called Kinjika. There was no doubt about it, the man was dying. But why? Although he was in great pain and even greater agony of mind, the medical profession could find no name for his illness. A battery of tests and treatments produced no results. Helpless, they looked on as he sank further and further from life. On the fifth day after his arrival, he died.

The man had been flown from his native Arnhem Land in the Northern Territories and had been a member of the Mailli people. What happened to him was closely connected to his origins and beliefs.

It seems that Kinjika acted against one of the taboos of his people concerning which women he was permitted to consider as possible partners. These rules are strict and deeply felt, but Kinjika went his own way. In a sense, that was the beginning of the process that would bring about his death. When he was summoned by the tribal council, knowing that he had no defence for his actions, he refused to attend. A sentence of death was pronounced upon him in his absence.

In a movie, hit men might have been hired to hunt him down and do the job and, in a way, that is what happened. But the hit men in question carried no guns and wielded no knives. What they had with them was a killing bone, called a *kundela*, and it had the power of the whole tribe behind it.

In a complicated ceremony, closed to women and anyone outside the tribe, the *kundela* was charged with a deadly energy. Between six and nine inches long, sanded smooth and with a plait of hair attached to one end, the bone might come from an emu, a kangaroo, or even a human. The men entrusted with this powerful object are called *kurdaitcha*. They usually work in twos or threes and wear a traditional and fearsome costume. Slippers made from cockatoo feathers and human hair leave no trail upon the ground. The hunters' skins are painted with human blood, to which kangaroo hair is stuck. Masks of emu feathers complete the terrifying picture.

These *kurdaitcha* are said never to give up. They will track their quarry for years if need be, but they will get him in the end. When they find the condemned man, they do not even touch him. Dropping to one knee, they point the sharpened end of the *kundela* at the victim and thrust it towards him, crying out a ritual chant in a high, piercing tone. Then they simply leave and return to their people. The *kundela's* work is done. It is burnt, never to be used again.

This is what happened to Kinjika. From that day he was doomed. As is the custom, not a single friend or member of his family would talk to him or acknowledge him. In the street, they looked through him. In his home, they did not prepare food for him or admit to his presence in any way. They treated him as if he were dead already. He was in the American phrase used of prisoners to be executed "a dead man walking". Such a state can go on for days or even weeks, but the outcome is inevitable. Sooner or later, the condemned man weakens and dies. Often, as was the case with Kinjika, the medical profession is puzzled to explain what is happening.

Is it fear that kills? Is it the sense that all your people have condemned you? Is it the feeling of desolation that occurs when everyone you know and love looks through you, as if you are already gone from the everyday world? Is it the condemned man's own sense of guilt, given concrete form by the pointing bone, that finally destroys him?

Death comes to all of us. It is the one certain fact of our lives. In modern times, the idea of someone being cursed and dying as a result seems absurd, yet the power of the human mind and spirit over the body is well established in medical literature. Time and again, doctors see dying patients who, against the odds, are determined to survive until a special date or until they have seen a loved one. When what the patient longs for has occurred, he or she seems somehow to be ready for death ... and death comes. Perhaps that is what happens when the condemned man looks up and sees the *kurdaitcha* kneeling before him. The will to live departs and then it is only a matter of time.

The belief that the uttering of certain words or the doing of ritual actions can bring about harm to another human being is deep-seated in many cultures around the world. At times in history, those believed to be able to curse or bewitch others have themselves been persecuted. Thousands of so-called witches have been burnt at the stake or otherwise executed. Most of them were probably harmless eccentrics but, as we have seen in this story, the belief that someone or something can do you harm may help to make that a reality. Perhaps some witches were dangerous after all.

The Barbarous Barber

In eighteenth-century London, the apprehension of criminals was a pretty hit-and-miss affair. No doubt in the narrow, dark, stinking back streets of the capital, countless crimes were committed that never saw the light of day. But for a man embarking on the killing of hundreds of people, disposing of the bodies was a serious issue. Such a man was Sweeney Todd, a barber in Fleet Street. His solution was effective and horrifying.

Todd had a rough upbringing and was in prison before he was twenty. Later, he set himself up as a barber and eventually bought premises in Fleet Street. Whether he did so because of their "original features" is not known. Below Todd's barber shop was a basement. From this dark, damp hole, Todd could gain access to the crypts and tunnels beneath nearby St Dunstan's Church, and from these, he could gain access to another shop, run by a certain Mrs Lovett. It was a bakery shop, famous for the quality of its meat pies.

The scene is horrible to imagine. A passer-by enters Todd's shop, looking for a close shave before an important meeting. There is no one else in the shop, which consists only of a bare room with a barber's chair in the middle. In those days, barbers did more than cut hair and shave, they also took out teeth, let blood, and wove human hair into wigs, so they were not, by nature, a squeamish bunch.

The barber's client settles down in the chair and leans back comfortably. Like hairdressers all over the world, Todd, a pale-faced, red-haired little sprite of a man, engages the client in small talk. Has he come far? What is his line of work? In such a situation, customers tend to talk. In this case, it is a big mistake. The man confides that he is a sailor, newly arrived, and on an important mission to take something of importance to his master. Do Todd's eyes gleam for a moment in the dimly-lit shop?

He looks towards the door to make sure that no one is about to enter, then, in a swift move, he presses a lever with his foot.

Clang! The chair swings down as a trapdoor revolves. The other side of the trapdoor comes to the top, and it, too, has a barber's chair upon it. Within a second, all is as normal in Todd's shop, but someone has disappeared from the face of the earth.

Todd doesn't waste a second. The drop to the floor of the basement below is quite far, but men have been known to survive more. Quickly, he grabs a lamp and runs down the stairs, making sure to take his sharpest straight-bladed razor with him. The basement is foul. By the flickering light, a heap in the middle of the floor is revealed as the body of the unfortunate sailor. Was that a groan? Todd passes the razor swiftly across the man's neck. All is certainly silent now.

But Todd still has work to do. Quickly, he searches the man (and finds the valuable pearls he was carrying), then he strips him. Next, he drags the body into the vaults of St Dunstan's. No one will disturb him here, for they were sealed years ago. There is more work for the razor. With a skill born of years of practice, he begins to strip the flesh from the man's bones, removing the skin but putting the internal organs to one side. Before long, several boxes of meat and offal are neatly packed and ready for transport to the baker's shop on the other side of the vaults. Only one problem remains. A pile of bloody bones, skin and a horrifically mutilated skull remain on the floor. Todd searches for a hiding place. Most of the monuments down here already have rotting remains tucked behind them, although the original burials were long, long ago. Todd pushes aside the lid of an ornate coffin. Inside, the shroud has long since caved into the dessicated chest of the occupant. There is plenty of room. Todd piles in these latest remains of his own and pushes on the lid.

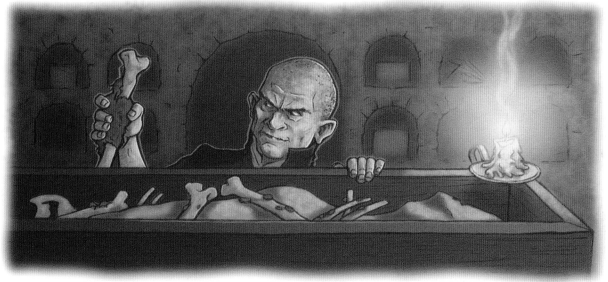

At the pie shop of Mrs Lovett, a woman after Todd's own heart, the midday rush has just begun. Mrs Lovett's pies are renowned on both sides of the river. The flesh is delicate and well-seasoned. The gravy is rich and succulent. At noon, when the first batch comes out of the oven, there is always a queue. Todd leaves his boxes unobtrusively at the rear and hurries back to his shop. He may be losing custom.

The Demon Barber of Fleet Street got away with his foul crimes for years. Several circumstances led to his eventual downfall. Stories began to go around the streets that more customers entered a certain barber's shop than ever left it. Then there was the smell in St Dunstan's church. Even the vicar had to hold a handkerchief to his nose as he gave his sermon, Investigations were made. At first, the evidence was far from conclusive. but a search of Sweeney Todd's premises revealed a number of articles of value, and some of them could be traced to people who had gone missing over preceding months, saying they might just drop into the barber's on their way.

Todd's trial made front-page news. Mrs Lovett, however, decided not to await the hangman's attentions. She poisoned herself in prison. The jury took only five minutes to make up its mind. Todd was sentenced to death and hanged in 1802.

Many people felt safer that night, but they did not rest easy. They could never forget quite how many of Mrs Lovett's delicious pies they had enjoyed in the past.

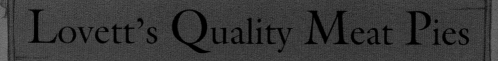

Lovett's Quality Meat Pies

~Lovett's Pies~

Sweeney Todd's success as a murderer was largely because he had means and opportunity. It must have seemed to him as if victims positively offered themselves up to him as they lay back in his chair. He had a motive, too – greed. Todd grew up in the filthy slums of London. His parents were alcoholics who, one cold winter's night, went out in search of gin and never returned. They probably froze to death, too drunk to understand the danger. But not everyone who grew up in those conditions became a mass murderer. It's a problem that remains with us to this day. Exactly why do some men turn to good and others to evil?

The Legend of Sleepy Hollow

On the eastern shores of the Hudson River lies the little port of Greensburgh, although many call it Tarry Town because of the willingness of local men to tarry in the taverns there on market day. Not more than two miles inland is a secluded valley, surrounded by high hills and with a brook running through it – one of the most peaceful places in all the world. It is known as Sleepy Hollow, and there is a drowsy, dreamy feeling about the place that seems to make the inhabitants particularly likely to see strange and extraordinary things, from ghosts to goblins to wonders in the sky.

In this quiet corner lived a schoolmaster by the name of Ichabod Crane. He was tall and thin, with narrow shoulders, long arms and legs, hands that dangled out of his sleeves, and feet like shovels. His head was small and flat on top, with huge ears, large green, glassy eyes, and a long nose. Stalking along, with his clothes flapping around him, he looked just like a scarecrow.

The one-room building where Ichabod taught the local children was not a very attractive edifice. It was built of logs and, although there were shutters, only some of the windows had glass in them. The rest were patched with the leaves of old copy-books. A huge birch tree grew at one end, and a stream ran beside the schoolroom, which was some way from any other building.

The schoolroom was not suitable to live in, so, as was the custom at the time, Ichabod stayed with the parents of his pupils, moving from one home to the next week by week, with all his worldly goods tied up in a cotton handkerchief. It was not in his interests to become a nuisance to those who gave him his livelihood, so the schoolmaster found various ways of being useful to the families he visited. He helped on the farms and was remarkably good with small children. He was also the singing master for the area, and regularly led a small choir in the village church.

In a small, rural community, the schoolmaster is considered to be almost as learned as the parson. He made the local lads seem rough and unworldly. He was often surrounded by a bevy of beauties, while their male counterparts hung back and muttered. Apart from anything else, by moving from home to home as he did, Ichabod was a wonderful source of gossip and therefore very popular with the ladies.

The schoolmaster was, however, terribly susceptible to the tales of hauntings and horrors that abounded in that region. His finest book was a history of New England witchcraft, and, as he walked home in the dark each evening, he had no difficulty in imagining that every little sound was a ghoul or a goblin. His quavering voice could often be heard through the gloom as he sang psalms to keep his spirits up.

Of course, the good women of the area enjoyed a frightening tale as much as he did. As he sat at their firesides by night, they delighted to feed his appetite for haunted ditches and bewitched buildings. The most terrifying tale of all concerned the headless horseman, said to be the ghost of a Hessian trooper. It was told that, during a battle in the War of Independence, a cannon ball carried away his head. Although his body was laid to rest in the churchyard, his spirit rides abroad each night in search of the missing head, and, anxious to finish his mission before daybreak, he dashes through the valley like an ice-cold blast. The name he is usually given is the Headless Horseman of Sleepy Hollow. So it was, that, as he walked home at night, Ichabod Crane's blood was chilled by any gusting wind, and he made it a point never to look behind him as he hurried on his way.

Ichabod Crane's undoing (and the undoing of many another man) was, as you may guess, a woman. She was the daughter of a very prosperous Dutch farmer, and she came each week to join the schoolmaster's singing class. Her name was Katrina Van Tassel and, at eighteen, she was plump and fair, with a peachy complexion and rosy cheeks. She was pretty and she knew it. She dressed in a curious mixture of modern and old-fashioned clothes, all chosen carefully to show off her figure. All her necklaces were pure gold, inherited from her great-great-grandmother, Her petticoats were enticingly short, designed to show off the prettiest foot and the daintiest ankle for many a mile.

Ichabod's enthusiasm for this enchanting creature, the only child of her father, was only heightened when he visited her home and saw for himself the prosperity of her family. The thriving farm was situated beside the Hudson River and everything spoke of wealth not-too-ostentatiously enjoyed. Beside the pretty farmhouse, a huge barn was filled to capacity. There were fertile, green meadows, and rich fields of wheat, rye, buckwheat and Indian corn as well as orchards heavy with ripe fruit. In Ichabod's mind's eye, he could see the farm sold and himself, with Katrina and several charming children, setting off in a covered wagon for Kentucky, Tennessee or wherever else a vast acreage might be purchased with even a little money.

Inside, the dwelling was just as enticing: a treasure house of the fruits and beauties of the earth, from strings of dried apples and peaches to ostrich eggs and treasures of old silver. From the moment Ichabod saw all these delights, his peace of mind was at an end. He could think only of how to win the daughter of the house.

It was not going to be easy. Apart from the character of the lady herself, which was full of whims and caprices, Ichabod had to contend with many rivals in love. Several local lads were equally smitten by Katrina's charms, but one above all caused Ichabod concern. His name was Abraham Van Brunt, but he was known throughout the surrounding region – for his fame had spread far and wide – as Brom Bones. This brawny young man, with curly black hair and handsome face, was renowned for his exploits. He was famed for great knowledge and skill in horsemanship, prodigious feats of strength, winning races and, by dint of his superior size and weight, settling disputes. He was always ready for a fight or for fun, and although full of the arrogance of youth, he was, at bottom, a good-hearted fellow. Together with three or four close companions, he scandalized the aged population and made them smile at the same time. Whenever any mischief was done, it was pretty sure that Brom Bones was at the bottom of it.

For some time now, Brom Bones had set his cap at the fair Katrina, and it was whispered that she was not entirely averse to his attentions, although they certainly lacked finesse. His peers feared to cross young Brom and discreetly withdrew, never daring to call upon Katrina when the young cavalier's horse was tied up outside.

Ichabod Crane knew that he had a fearsome rival but he was not dismayed. With perseverance he pursued his aim, visiting the house frequently in his role as singing teacher and happy in the knowledge that Katrina's parents did not appear to be against the match. Pretty soon,

Brom Bones found his position as leading suitor in question. His horse was no longer seen tied outside the farmhouse on Sunday evenings, and in his heart a deadly feud arose between himself and the schoolmaster.

If Brom Bones had had his way, the matter would have been settled in a gentlemanlike manner … by single combat. Ichabod, however, knew only too well how *that* would turn out. He avoided Brom and never rose to his challenges, which frustrated the young pretender very much. Brom was left to mock his rival, even teaching a little dog to whine in a way that fitted her, he said, to become a replacement for Katrina's current singing teacher.

All this went on for some time. Then, one afternoon in autumn, Ichabod was sitting in his schoolroom watching his scholars attempting to concentrate on their books, when a servant of Farmer Van Tassel's arrived with an invitation for Ichabod to attend an evening of merry-making that very day.

Ichabod's heart quickened. In no time at all, he had rushed his pupils through their lessons and hurried them out of the door. He then spent a long time getting ready, brushing his one black suit, arranging his hair as he peered into an old broken piece of mirror, and even going so far as to borrow a horse from the farmer with whom he was currently staying. True, it was only a broken-down plough-horse, as gaunt and gangling as its rider, but its name was Gunpowder, so it must have had some fire and mettle in its day.

Ichabod felt himself to be a knight riding forth to meet his lady, but the picture he presented to the casual onlooker was rather different. He rode with short stirrups, bringing his knees much nearer to his chin than was wise, and his elbows stuck out to the side like a grasshopper's. His whip was carried like a sceptre, and he wore a small wool hat on the front of his head.

On this fine autumn day, with trees in varying dresses from green to russet, Ichabod's mind, as he rode, roamed over the treasures being gathered into the Van Tassel's barns: apples, Indian corn, yellow pumpkins and buckwheat.

It was towards evening that Ichabod arrived to find the Van Tassel residence thronging with young and old from all around. Prominent among them was Brom Bones himself who had ridden there on his famous steed Daredevil, a creature that no one but he could manage.

Inside, visions of beauty met Ichabod's gaze on every side. Buxom wenches vied for his attention with tables groaning with delicious baked goods. There were pies and cakes of every description, not to mention roasted chickens, bowls of milk and cream, slices of ham and smoked beef, and dishes of peaches, plums and pears.

Ichabod ate his fill, fondly considering how fine his life would be if all of this were his, until he heard music strike up next door. Now Ichabod loved to dance almost as much as he loved to sing. In seconds, he was flying and flapping about the dance floor, his beloved in his arms, and pleasantly conscious of Brom Bones glowering in the corner.

After the dancing, Ichabod was drawn to a group of the older folk, surrounding Farmer Van Tassel. They were telling stories of the old days, of wars and of wonders. Naturally, the talk turned to ghost stories, and many extraordinary tales were told of wailings and cries, of the woman in white who haunted the dark glen at Raven Rock, of funeral trains and dismal hauntings. But most talk was of the Headless Horseman, of course, who nightly tethered his horse in the churchyard of Sleepy Hollow.

This church stood on a knoll, surrounded by locust-trees and lofty elms. On one side of the whitewashed church was a wide, woody dell, along which a large brook bubbled among rocks and fallen trees. Over a deep part of the stream was a wooden bridge, thickly shaded by overhanging trees. By day it was a cool and melancholy place. By night it was fearfully dark. Here it was that the headless horseman was said to linger, and a tale was told of an old man who had been thrown into the brook by the frolicsome spectre. Brom Bones had to cap this story, and told how he himself had met the galloping ghost and challenged him to a race. "I would have won, too," he said, "for Daredevil was more than a match for his goblin horse, but just as we came to the church bridge, the horseman vanished in a flash of fire!"

Ichabod Crane joined in the conversation, adding his own spooky stories from his history of witchcraft. By the time the party broke up, Ichabod was feeling full of himself and ready to press his suit upon his beloved. No one knows how his interview with the lady went, but it was not an obviously happy man who shortly afterwards led out his horse and urged it homeward with a number of vicious kicks and cuffs.

So it was that, in no very good frame of mind, Ichabod Crane rode home at midnight, through a countryside that seemed unnaturally silent

and still. All the stories of ghosts and goblins he had heard that evening came crowding into his mind. He jumped at every broken twig, shivered at the groaning of the branches overhead, and trembled at every rustle in the undergrowth.

Suddenly, as it arrived at a small bridge, Ichabod's horse stood stock still. Ichabod jerked the reins and kicked the horse but to no avail. Just at that moment, he heard a slight splashing sound and, looking up, saw something dark and misshapen, towering in the midst of the dark grove. The hair on the schoolmaster's head rose up in horror. It was too late to run. Summoning all his courage, he cried out in a quavering voice, "Who are you?" There was no reply, but the shape suddenly bunched itself together and sprang on to the road in front of Ichabod. It was a horseman of huge size, mounted on a powerful black horse. He did not acknowledge the presence of Ichabod Crane, but jogged along on the opposite side of the road, keeping abreast of him. Ichabod tried his usual trick of singing psalms to keep his spirits up, but his tongue seemed to get stuck in his mouth, and no sound emerged. He could not tear his eyes away from the image beside him, and it was with a kind of sick horror that he realized for the first time that the horseman appeared to have no head on his shoulders, but was holding one in front of him on the saddle.

Once again, Ichabod urged his mount, and this time, Gunpowder leapt into the air and dashed off down the hill. The spectre kept pace with him as Ichabod clung on for dear life. Luck was not with him. As they approached the church, gleaming white through the trees, Ichabod felt his girth slipping and his saddle giving way. By flinging his arms around Gunpowder's neck, he managed to keep his seat while the saddle slipped to the ground right under the hoofs of his pursuer.

The church bridge was fast approaching. If Ichabod could just hang on, this was where the headless horseman might disappear. Ichabod glanced over his shoulder and saw to his horror that the horseman was raising the severed head in front of him and about to throw the ghastly object. Ichabod tried to dodge, but it was too late. The missile hit his own head with a horrible crash. He was thrown to the ground, while the black horse, the ghostly rider and Gunpowder passed by like a whirlwind.

Next morning, the horse was found, without its saddle, calmly cropping grass outside its owner's gate. Of the schoolmaster there was no sign. Later in the day, some villagers set out to search for the missing man. When they came to the church, they saw the marks of many hoofs in the mud, the hat of the unfortunate Ichabod, and close beside it a shattered pumpkin. No further trace of Ichabod Crane was found. The general opinion was clear: Ichabod Crane had been carried off by the Headless Horseman.

In time, another schoolmaster came to do duty in the Hollow, and Ichabod was all but forgotten. After a few months, Brom Bones conducted Katrina Van Tassel to the altar.

Several years later, an old farmer who had visited New York, brought back the news that Ichabod Crane was alive and well in another part of the country. He had been to college, studied law, been admitted to the bar, become a politician, written for the newspapers and finally been made a magistrate. The old country wives, however, knew better. They were sure that Ichabod Crane had been spirited away by supernatural means. The bridge by the church became an even greater source of fear, and the old schoolhouse (for a new one was now in use) was said to be haunted by the ghost of the gangling pedagogue. Only Brom Bones always burst into a hearty laugh when the pumpkin found next to Ichabod's hat was mentioned, which led some to believe that he knew more about the matter than he chose to tell.

Humour and horror may seem starnge companions, but the pairing makes sense. Just as medical students joke over the bodies they are dissecting to dispel the ghastliness of the situation, so horror films have long used laughter to relieve the tension in a gruesome story. Then, when the viewer is relaxed again, the true terror can begin. The famous story retold here is by Washington Irving, an American author who died in 1859 and was also responsible for bringing us Rip Van Winkle.

The Devil's Bargain

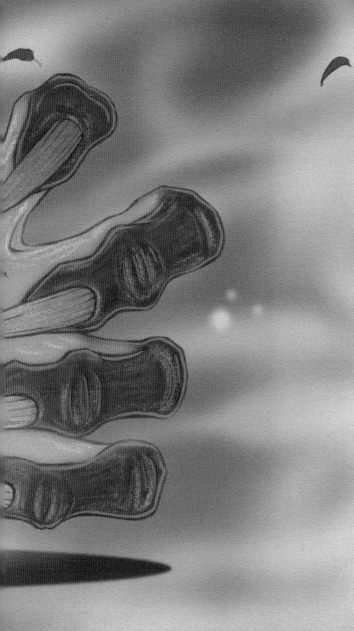

In Weimar, Germany, a boy named Johann Faustus grew up in a decent, God-fearing household. He was clever and avidly studied whatever was put before him. Before long, theology, medicine and mathematics were not enough. He delved into sorcery, prophecy and astrology. Soon Faustus's pride filled him with ambition and a desire for power. He was determined to challenge the Devil himself.

One night, Dr Faustus, as he now was, journeyed secretly to a forest near Wittenberg, where, drawing circles on the ground, he summoned the Devil.

A great storm blew up. Mighty winds whipped the branches and lightning flashed through the sky. In the midst of the whirling wind, the Devil appeared, apparently furious at being called by a mere mortal.

The storm subsided, and so did the Devil's rage. He asked with chilling quietness what Dr Faustus desired.

"I am willing to make a bargain with you," said the scholar. There was no limit to his outrageous pride. "It has three parts. First, you will serve me as long as I live. Second, you will tell me whatever I wish to know. Third, you must never lie to me."

"This bargain is a little one-sided," hissed the Devil. "I, too, have three conditions. First, after twenty-four years, you will surrender your body and soul to me. Second, you will sign a written version of our agreement in your own blood. Third, you will renounce your Christian faith."

Dr Faustus agreed. Who knows if he hesitated as he took this fearful step and, dipping a pen into his own blood by the light of the moon, sealed his fate.

It was a very different life that Faustus enjoyed thereafter. He could have anything he liked. His life was filled with comfort and luxury. The most exquisite foods, the most delicious wines, the most beautiful women graced his table and his bed. Yet nothing was ever enough.

Faustus gained fame, too, as the most renowned astrologer of his day. His predictions always came true, for the Devil showed him whatever he wished to know. Nor was he bound by the earth itself. With his satanic master, he went from the depths of hell to the farthest reaches of space. The universe itself was his playground.

But at the back of Faustus's mind, a small, insistent voice began to speak. It reminded him that time was passing, and as the years went by, the voice became louder and louder. Twenty-four years seems forever to a young man. To one in his middle years, it is no longer so. Faustus grew more and more melancholy as the date of his doom approached. Even his enjoyment of everything that his bargain had brought him seemed to leave him. None of it mattered, when there was so little time to live. Indeed, not only life but his immortal soul was soon to be sacrificed. Faustus bequeathed all his worldly possessions to one of his students.

In his final months, Faustus was a changed man. All around could see that he was ill. On the evening of the last day of the twenty-fourth year, seeing that his spirits had reached unparalleled depths, they gathered at his house.

Soon after midnight, an unearthly noise came from Dr Faustus's room. No one dared to enter as a sound like a mighty tempest roared inside. Then there was shouting – terrifying screams that shook the house, then grew fainter and fainter, until there was no sound at all.

It was daybreak before the students dared to enter their teacher's room. The sight that met their eyes in the dim light of dawn was horrifying beyond belief.

The room was splattered with blood. Fragments of brain and teeth clung to the walls and hangings. Outside, what remained of Faustus's body, warm and still convulsively twitching, was stretched over a manure heap.

No one who was there that day ever recovered from the horrors they had seen, but many took it as a sign to hold fast to the ways of God, for the ways of the Devil are terrible indeed.

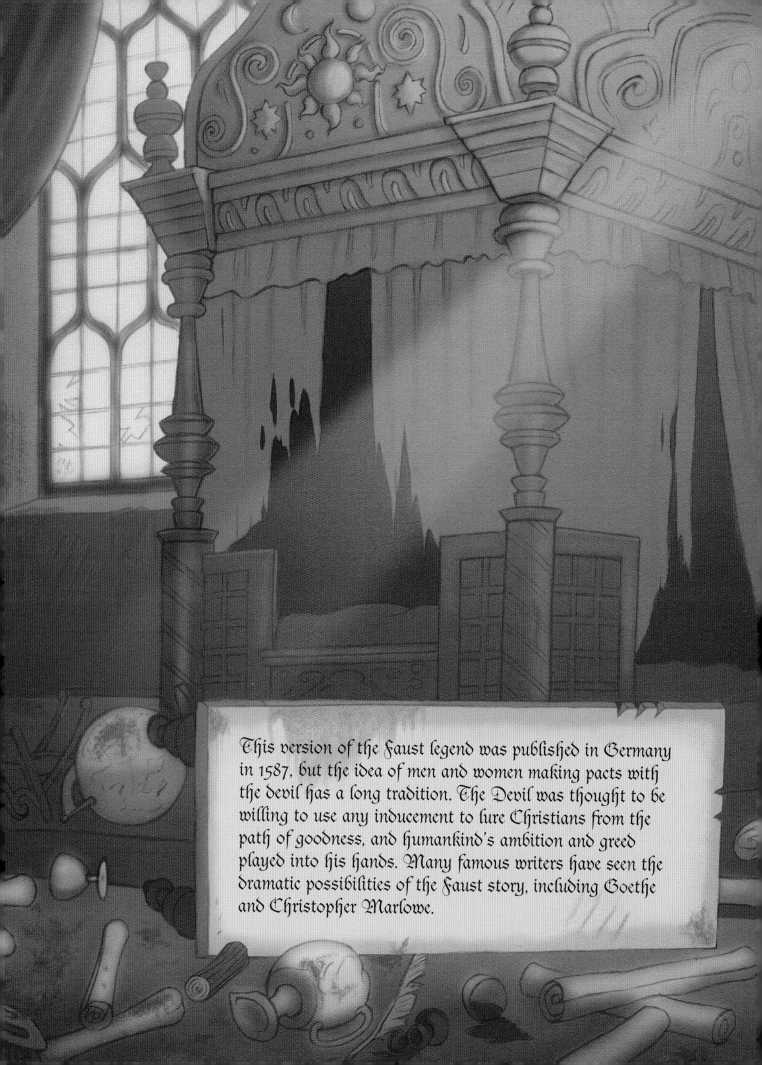

This version of the Faust legend was published in Germany in 1587, but the idea of men and women making pacts with the devil has a long tradition. The Devil was thought to be willing to use any inducement to lure Christians from the path of goodness, and humankind's ambition and greed played into his hands. Many famous writers have seen the dramatic possibilities of the Faust story, including Goethe and Christopher Marlowe.

The Hound of the Baskervilles

It was one October morning that the great detective Sherlock Holmes was visited in his rooms in Baker Street, London, by a very tall, thin man, with a long nose like a beak, two keen dark eyes, gold-rimmed glasses and a rather dishevelled appearance. In fact, the visitor had already called on the previous evening, when the detective was away, and had absent-mindedly left his stick behind. Using his famous powers of deduction upon this item, Holmes had already correctly deduced that the man was a country doctor by the name of James Mortimer.

Meeting Holmes face to face, the doctor rapidly came to the point of his visit. He lived, it seemed, on Dartmoor, in Devon, a curiously wild and desolate place. His problem, he said, was most urgent, but first he must read to the assembled company (for Holmes's great friend Doctor Watson was, as usual, present) two documents. The first, an old manuscript dating from 1742, told a strange and disturbing tale. It related the events leading to the death of a man named Sir Hugo Baskerville. This man, it seemed, was the local squire, living at Baskerville Hall. However, his reputation caused most local people to fear rather than to respect him. Sir Hugo conceived a passion for a girl whose father owned a little land bordering the Baskerville estate. The young woman, being of good character and having heard many sordid tales about the squire, avoided him. This, if anything, inflamed her suitor even more. One evening, accompanied by a group of his drinking companions and knowing that her father and brothers were away from home, Sir Hugo rode over to the farm, seized the girl, and carried her back to the Hall, where he locked her in an upstairs room.

Below, the terrified girl could hear sounds of revelry and increasing drunkenness as Sir Hugo and his friends made merry. The oaths and curses that floated up from the floor below made the girl more frightened than ever for her safety. At last, able to bear it no longer, she climbed from the window and set off on her own across the moor, heading for her father's house.

A little later, Sir Hugo discovered that his captive was missing. Bellowing with rage, he leapt on to the massive table in the great hall and vowed that the Devil could take him, body and soul, that very evening if he could overtake the girl. He rode from the Hall with his hunting dogs in full cry behind him, and followed the path the girl must have taken across the moonlit moor.

At first Sir Hugo's companions did not know what to do. It was only when a few of them had sobered a little that they rode off in pursuit of their leader. On the way, they asked a shepherd if he had seen Sir Hugo and the pack, but the man reported glimpsing only one man, riding like the wind on a black mare, with an animal like a hound of Hell at his heels. Some of the group felt afraid, but they rode on, more cautiously now, until they came to the beginning of a deep valley in the moor. Here they found the hounds, some of them whimpering and cowering. Down in the valley, a horrific sight met the eyes of the three riders brave enough to ride on. The moon shone brightly on two ancient standing stones in a clearing. Between them lay the body of the young woman, dead of fear and fatigue. Nearby lay the earthly remains of Hugo Baskerville, but it was not this that terrified the onlookers. Standing over Hugo was an enormous hound, a great, black beast, which, before their eyes, ripped out the nobleman's throat. One look at the blazing eyes and dripping jaws of the animal sent the men screaming on their way. None of them ever recovered from the hellish sight.

Such was the content of the first document. "The coming of the hound is said to have plagued the family ever since," read Dr Mortimer. "Their deaths have been sudden and mysterious."

The doctor then turned to the second document, dated only five months before. It was a newspaper article telling of the death of the most recent owner of the Baskerville estate: Sir Charles Baskerville. An elderly gentleman without children, he had been a great benefactor in the area, and he was genuinely mourned. However, it was the manner of his death

that caused most interest. One evening, he went for his usual walk along the yew alley in the grounds of Baskerville Hall, smoking a cigar. When he had not returned by midnight, servants searched and found him, without a mark on his body, lying dead in the alley. Dr Mortimer had been a friend of Sir Charles, as well as his doctor. The baronet's heart had been weak, but still, the death was unexpected. What had not been reported in the press, but had been seen by Dr Mortimer himself when he examined the body, was the presence of footprints a few yards away.

"A man's or a woman's?" asked Holmes.

"Mr Holmes, they were the footprints of a gigantic hound!" the doctor replied.

There was only one gate leading from the yew alley, giving access to the moor. It seemed that Sir Charles had stood there for a while, looking out across the moor. Then he had seen someone or something that made him run – run for his life – towards the end of the alley. Sir Charles had been interested in the family legend and was afraid to venture upon the moor at night. Had the curse caught up with him after all?

Holmes reminded his guest that he had described the problem as urgent. Dr Mortimer replied that Henry Baskerville, Sir Charles's nephew and the last of the family, was due to arrive in London from Canada in just over an hour. What should he do?

Holmes stated that he would like to meet Sir Henry. The next morning, Holmes, Watson, Dr Mortimer and Sir Henry met in Baker Street. Already, there were strange events to report. The young man had received a letter, all except the last word cut from a newspaper. It said, "As you value your life or your reason keep away from the moor." In addition, one of his boots had been stolen from the hotel. Holmes also discovered that the heir was being followed by a man with a black beard.

Holmes advised that the young man should travel to Devon with Dr Mortimer as planned. Holmes himself had work in London, but Dr Watson could accompany the travellers to Baskerville Hall and remain there, reporting back to the famous detective, and making sure that Sir Henry never ventured on to the moor after dark.

Certainly, the first sight that Sir Henry and Watson had of Baskerville Hall was gloomy. Their spirits were not improved by the news that a convicted murderer had escaped from a nearby prison and was at loose upon the moor. The household was a small one, consisting only of Sir Henry and three servants who had been there during Sir Charles's day. Barrymore, the butler, and his wife looked after the house. Perkins, the groom, took care of the stables. The nearest village was several miles away, but it was not long before Sir Henry made the acquaintance of his nearest neighbour, Stapleton the naturalist, who lived with his very beautiful sister at Merripit House. The brooding moor, surrounding them on every side, had its own dangers and mysteries. Bogs could suck down the unwary traveller, while curious circular walls were the remains of ancient houses lived in by the prehistoric occupants of the region.

Watson did his best to keep Holmes informed by letter of all that happened. Together with Sir Henry, he discovered that someone was signalling from the Hall at night. It seemed that Mrs Barrymore was the sister of the escaped convict and was sending him food to his hiding place on the moor. Meanwhile, Sir Henry was rapidly falling in love with the fascinating Miss Stapleton. Watson felt full of foreboding but determined to do his duty, even when he became aware one night that another man was also hiding on the moor. Once or twice, a sound like the baying of a great hound was heard across those desolate reaches.

In an atmosphere of mounting tension, events began to move with ever quickening pace towards their end. Barrymore confided in Watson that on the night of his death, Sir Charles was due to meet a woman with the initials L.L. in the grounds. Watson doggedly discovered her to be a Mrs Laura Lyons. Married to a man who treated her badly and then left her, Mrs Lyons had been helped by several of the more wealthy people of the area, including Sir Charles. Determined to find out more, Watson visited the lady and found her to be beautiful but mysterious. She admitted to the appointment but claimed that she had not kept it, refusing to say why. Later, Watson was told that a close relationship existed between Mrs Lyons and Stapleton of Merripit House.

Watson knew that he was supposed to keep an eye on Sir Henry, but the opportunity to find out more about the watcher on the moor drew him to follow a young lad who was clearly taking food to the stranger. He tracked him to one of the ancient stone buildings, where there were clear signs that someone had been camping. Clutching his revolver, Watson determined to wait in the gathering gloom until the mysterious man returned. At last he heard a footstep outside, and a voice.

"It is a lovely evening, my dear Watson. I really think that you will be more comfortable outside than in."

It was Sherlock Holmes, who had come to maintain his own secret vigil. He was convinced that great danger lay ahead for Sir Henry Baskerville. Watson was astonished to learn from Holmes that the beautiful woman at Merripit House was Stapleton's wife, not his sister. It seemed that Stapleton was a much more sinister figure than had at first appeared. "My nets are closing upon him," said Holmes.

In the growing darkness, Holmes and Watson were startled by a dreadful repeated scream, echoing across the moor. The baying of a great hound added a new horror. The pair ran towards the sound. "He has beaten us, Watson. We are too late!" cried Holmes, as they came across a blood-spattered body in Sir Henry's familiar clothes.

It was only when Holmes leant over the body that he realized the truth. It was Selden, the escaped convict, who had been supplied with some of Sir Henry's old clothes. At the next moment, Stapleton himself appeared. When he realized that the body was not that of Sir Henry, he had to struggle to keep his composure. Knowing that

Henry Baskerville was due to dine with Stapleton the following evening, Holmes mentioned that had to return to London in the morning. He and Watson walked back to Baskerville Hall together.

Although Holmes had no doubt that Stapleton was responsible for the death, through fear, of Sir Charles Baskerville, and that he planned to murder Sir Henry, there was still no proof. Only a trap, with all the risks that this entailed, could bring Stapleton to justice. That evening, taking supper in the dining hall of Baskerville Hall, Holmes suddenly exclaimed at the sight of a portrait of bad, bold Sir Hugo of old. There was a distinct resemblance to the owner of Merripit House! Could Stapleton be a long lost cousin of Henry Baskerville, the son of Sir Charles's reprobate youngest brother? At last a motive for his plotting was clear.

Next day, Holmes and Watson pretended to leave for London but instead visited Laura Lyons. News that Stapleton was already married prompted the lady to reveal that it had, indeed, been he who persuaded her not to keep her appointment with Sir Charles Baskerville on the night of his death.

The moment of truth was fast approaching. Holmes had summoned Lestrade, a police detective from London, to be present as the trap closed around his foe. All present were armed as they took up their positions behind rocks by the path leading from Merripit House.

Holmes was anxious. A sinister fog was curling down the slopes, threatening to hide the house and the path from view. At last steps were heard upon the path. Sir Henry was clearly nervous, constantly looking over his shoulder. Suddenly another sound could be heard, coming towards him from the fog. An enormous, coal-black hound leapt into view, its mouth breathing fire, flames flickering around its coat, its eyes burning with an unearthly glare. Holmes and Watson fired together, but the hound leapt forward and bore Sir Henry down under its massive weight. Desperately, Holmes emptied his revolver into the savaging animal. Just in time, the hound rolled away, dead, leaving the baronet half dead with fright but otherwise unharmed.

On investigating the house, the party found Mrs Stapleton tied up, with signs of her husband's brutality upon her body. She knew that he kept the hound, gleaming with phosphorescent paint, in an old tin mine in the midst of the moor and had tried to prevent him from carrying out his plan.

No one could find their way across the moor on such a night. It was not until the next morning that Mrs Stapleton led the detectives to her husband's secret lair. There was no sign of him. It seemed likely that the moor itself had claimed him as he ran for his life.

Sir Arthur Conan Doyle wrote many stories featuring his detective Sherlock Holmes, of which this (here retold in a shorter version) is perhaps the most atmospheric. As in many horror stories, the place itself becomes almost a character in the tale, with the brooding moor presiding over the events that take place on it.